THE MOVIE STORYBOOK

Adapted by ALISON LOWENSTEIN and TOMAS PALACIOS

Based on the Screenplay by CHRISTOPHER L. YOST
and CHRISTOPHER MARKUS & STEPHEN McFEELY

Story by DON PAYNE and ROBERT RODAT

Produced by KEVIN FEIGE, p.g.a.

Directed by ALAN TAYLOR

Illustrated by RON LIM, CAM SMITH, and LEE DUHIG

All Rights Reserved. Published by Marvel Press, an imprint of Disney Book Group. No part of this book may be reproduced or transmitted in any form or by any means, electronic or mechanical, including photocopying, recording, or by any information storage and retrieval system, without written permission from the publisher. For information address Marvel Press, 1101 Flower Street, Glendale, California 91201.

Printed in the United States of America

First Edition

1 3 5 7 9 10 8 6 4 2

Library of Congress Control Number: 2013936922

ISBN 978-1-4231-7272-7

TM & © 2013 MARVEL
marvelkids.com

SUSTAINABLE FORESTRY INITIATIVE · Certified Sourcing
www.sfiprogram.org
SFI-00993
This Label Applies to Text Stock Only

NEW YORK • LOS ANGELES

THE UNIVERSE WAS IN PERIL. Wars raged

across the cosmos. Even with a Super Hero like the Mighty Thor traveling from realm to realm battling monsters and villains in order to maintain peace, there was still something sinister brewing deep within space.

On a massive ship in the depths of the universe, the Dark Elf Malekith clenched his fists and looked up at the billions of stars overhead. With his trusted companion Algrim by his side, Malekith reflected on the damage that had come to his world centuries ago at the hands of Asgard. The Dark Elf vowed revenge for the atrocities that had befallen his people.

From a balcony, Malekith looked at the cavernous amphitheater lined with what seemed to be a never-ending world of Dark Elves hanging from pods, ready to be awoken and to serve their master.

Malekith cradled his elf mask in his hands as he looked out into the dark space that lay beyond the amphitheater. It was time. . . .

MEANWHILE, on the planet Vanaheim, an intense battle was taking place between the local Vanir and a group of gruesome monsters called the Marauders. Deep within a thick, green forest, a young Vanir woman attempted to escape from a half dozen of the Marauders. She ran as fast as she could, but they were just too quick, especially the ones on horseback!

The Vanir woman tripped and landed hard at the bottom of the embankment. When she turned over, there stood a Marauder, a smirk on his face as he raised his weapon, ready to strike.

Suddenly, a large mace smashed the creature in the chest, sending him flying through the air. The woman looked over to see her hero. It was Hogun the Grim, a member of the Warriors Three!

Hogun didn't come alone. Emerging on a white horse, Fandral fought off the Marauders with his gleaming sword. Soon, Lady Sif and Volstagg also joined in the fight. But the battle had been intense and the Warriors Three and Lady Sif had been fighting for days.

As the increasing number of Marauders closed in on them, they exchanged worried looks. They gathered up their last bit of strength and pushed back the Marauders, just for a few inches of breathing room. The Vanir cowering behind the warriors from Asgard closed their eyes. This was the end.

As the Marauders moved in for the final blow, a huge blinding light appeared behind them! The light was followed by a thunderous *KRA-KOOM!* It was the Bifrost, the bridge used by Asgardians to travel from realm to realm. The Bifrost beamed down, right on top of the Marauders!

CLING! CLONG! CLONG! Down went three Marauders as a strange object shot out of the Bifrost and smashed into each monster. Then the object stopped in midair. Lady Sif squinted to take a closer look at this baffling entity. She smiled, recognizing the leathery tassel that hung from its mythical handle. It was Mjolnir! The mighty hammer from Asgard! Mjolnir turned and flew back toward the Bifrost, and was caught by a powerful arm!

IT WAS THE MIGHTY THOR!

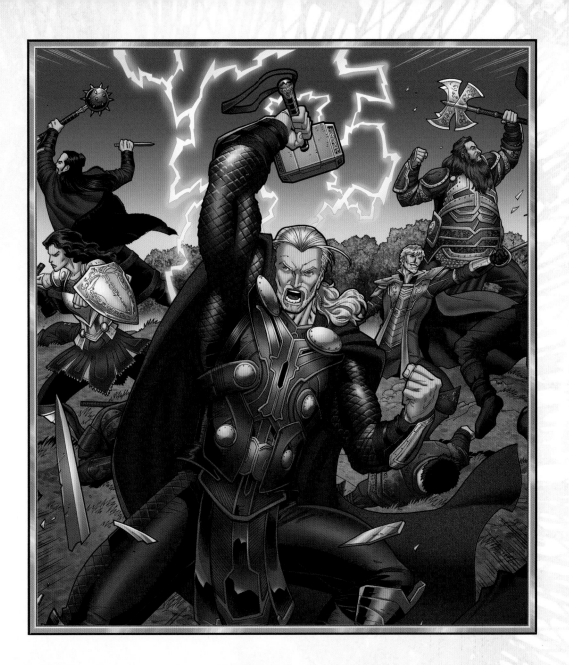

Thor was ready for whatever came his way. He nodded at his fellow Asgardians, and then, spinning Mjolnir, he unleashed an attack, raining down on the Marauders with power and thunder! The Warriors Three and Lady Sif joined in the attack as one by one the frightening creatures fell all around them.

Lady Sif wanted Thor to know that this was her battle. "I have this under control."

"Is that why everything is on fire?" Thor asked as he looked out at the smoke-filled forest.

"Think you can do better?" Lady Sif replied.

Before Thor could answer, a rumbling noise came from the forest, and then something leaped out and landed in front of them. Something huge. It was an enormous Kronan Stone Man! His presence seemed to block out the sun. This powerful beast wielded a metal club, which he held aloft as he stepped toward Thor.

The Marauders teemed with excitement at their secret weapon. Like spectators at a boxing match, they waited with nervous excitement, ready to watch the showdown.

Shaking his metal club high in the air, the Kronan giant leaped toward Thor. The gigantic man of stone tried to crush the warrior, but the god of thunder fought back!

The Kronan swung his club and Thor swung his mystical hammer. With one tremendous blow the two weapons clashed, and a loud crack rang out over the land of Vanaheim. Dust and debris filled the air, as everyone tried to look past the smoke and see who was still standing. When the dust settled, all that was left of the menacing stone man was his feet.

The Marauders were stunned! Their secret weapon was destroyed. They had no more tricks. They dropped their weapons and surrendered.

"Next time we should just start with the big one," Fandral joked.

Thor and his fellow Asgardian warriors had won the battle!

Sif and Fandral lined the Marauders up and placed manacles on their wrists. The people of Vanaheim heaved a sigh of relief as they watched the parade of failed soldiers marching through their village.

Smoke rose from the fields, as the Vanir people looked out at their burned planet. Despite the hardships, they would resume their lives and rebuild their encampment.

Hogun was helping a Vanir woman and her child when he glanced over and noticed Thor observing something off into the distance. Hogun walked over, showing he was ready to return to Asgard. But Thor thought otherwise.

"No. The peace is nearly won across the Nine Realms," Thor said as he looked over to the Vanir woman and child. "Your duty is to be where your heart is." They exchanged a nod of understanding, then shook hands. Thor turned, looked up to the stars, then called upon the one being who could open the Bifrost.

"Heimdall. When you are ready." And with that the Bifrost opened and everyone stepped inside.

BACK ON THE OTHER SIDE of the Bifrost lay Asgard. One of the Nine Realms of the cosmos, it was the land of a strong people, the Asgardians. Perched at the edge of the realm sat the Observatory. Its golden dome housed the Bifrost, the means by which the Mighty Thor and his fellow warriors traveled from realm to realm. Asgard was Thor's home, and this is what he protected.

Under the magnificent palace lay the Asgardian dungeon, home to some of the Nine Realms' most dangerous villains. The soldiers of Asgard, the Einherjar, led the shackled Marauders to the dim cells that were to be their new home.

The Marauders weren't alone in this dark prison. It was also home to the most famous prisoner of them all: Thor's trickster brother, Loki. As he watched the defeated creatures step into their cells, his only visitor arrived. No matter what he had done wrong, Loki's mother, Frigga, still came to see her son. She saw the good in Loki, even if others couldn't.

But he resented her. And his brother, for that matter. He felt they had abandoned him. Frigga sighed and closed her eyes. Then, she disappeared. She was just a hologram.

THOR CHECKED IN WITH HIS FATHER,

Odin Allfather, King of Asgard. Thor told Odin that peace had been brought back to the Nine Realms and all was well. Or was it?

Somewhere in space, Malekith and Algrim trekked through their darkened and poisoned planet of Svartalfheim. Malekith reminisced about how his wife and children would play on the land, which now lay in ruins. The Dark Elf took off his mask and turned to Algrim. "I will restore our world to its former splendor or I will breathe this poisoned air till it kills me."

In response, Algrim took off his own mask and took a deep breath, pain filling his eyes, his stance proud. They would avenge their people and destroy anything and everything that stood in their way.

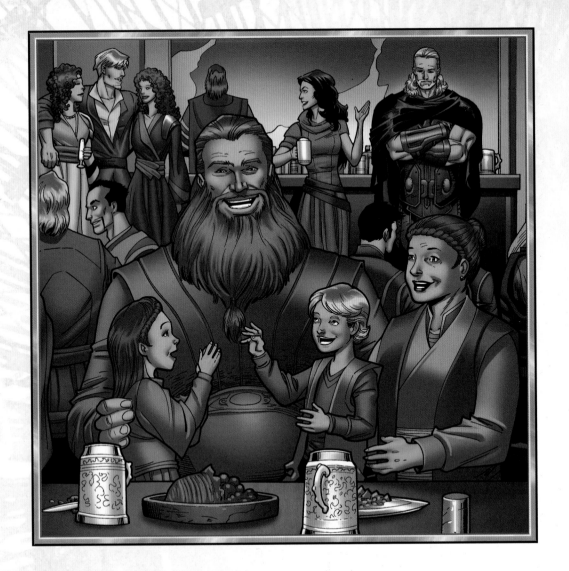

UNAWARE THAT MALEKITH was plotting a war, the Asgardians celebrated their victory against the Marauders. Everyone was having a great time, except for Thor. He was still heartbroken leaving the Earthling known as Jane. Although he was doing so much for the Nine Realms and was protecting so many people, he still missed his mortal love. He watched as Volstagg told the crowd the stories of their great accomplishments during battle. Thor lifted a tankard and drank with his fellow heroes. He was going to celebrate, and he had earned it! But his heart was simply not in it.

He went to see his friend Heimdall. He asked the all-seeing sentry if Jane was safe on Earth. Heimdall gazed at the stars and then turned to Thor. Something was not right with her.

MEANWHILE ON EARTH, Thor's old flame, Jane Foster, Darcy, and Darcy's intern, Ian, were racing through the streets of England tracking down a strange energy source that Jane's phase meter had picked up.

The phase meter tracked the energy to an old abandoned warehouse. Jane got out of the car to investigate. She found rusty metal shipping containers stacked up in an odd formation that she couldn't quite figure out. Yes, it was an odd sight, but nothing shocked Jane. Well, maybe that time she met a strange being from another realm and fell in love with him. She smiled. She knew she was on the brink of discovering something brilliant, and maybe reuniting with an old friend!

Jane stood in the middle of the decaying industrial complex and held on to the phase meter tightly. The readings were off the scale, and the meter was ringing louder and louder with every step she took.

Suddenly, a large gust of wind filled the room. Spots of black sand crept down the wall and piled in a corner, then disappeared into an invisible rift.

"Amazing," Jane said with wonder. Her hair waved in the wind, and she tried to keep the swirling black sand out of her face, when suddenly her shoes squeaked on the floor as her feet started sliding toward the doorway. She tried to stop, but she was pulled into the darkness!

Suddenly, a dark, swirling energy appeared before Jane. Wherever she moved, the energy appeared. Jane tried to fight this powerful force, but it was no use. Jane screamed, and then everything went black.

JANE AWOKE ON THE FLOOR of the complex.

What had happened? How long was she asleep? Was it all a dream? She made
her way outside, searching for Darcy and Ian. Jane saw them being questioned by
a police officer and ran toward Darcy. Instantly, the sky turned pitch-black and
heavy rain pounded down. Everyone was drenched . . . except Jane.

Large puddles of water surrounded Jane. Curious, she reached her arm out to feel
the rain, but not a single drop fell upon her. Jane gasped! It wasn't a dream! Half
a dozen soaking-wet policemen took a step back, unclear as to how this strange
phenomenon was happening. But it was about to get even stranger. Suddenly a
presence came over Jane. She looked down at her shadow, and another shadow
towered over hers. The police, Darcy, and Ian gasped! Jane turned, her eyes
wide! But then she relaxed and smiled at her old friend.

RETURNING HER SMILE,

Thor grabbed Jane and whisked her through the Bifrost as it fired down upon them. The fierce wind left debris flying about in a funnel shape, blowing a parking meter and a car hood through the sky, as Thor and Jane quickly disappeared.

They rushed through the space tunnel as the universe flew past them! Stars, planets, realms . . . all a zipping blur of magnificent colors! Thor tried to shield her, but Jane pushed his arm aside. She was a scientist and wanted to see everything! It was a fantastic sight.

Back on Svartalfheim, Malekith stood in front of his massive army. Hundreds of heavily armed elves, in their battle armor, stood ready, waiting for their leader's command. Algrim stood next to Malekith. The two Dark Elves looked at each other and nodded. It was time to seek revenge.

Malekith looked out, toward the universe, as if trying to pinpoint where Asgard was. A sinister grin came across his face. The battle was about to begin.

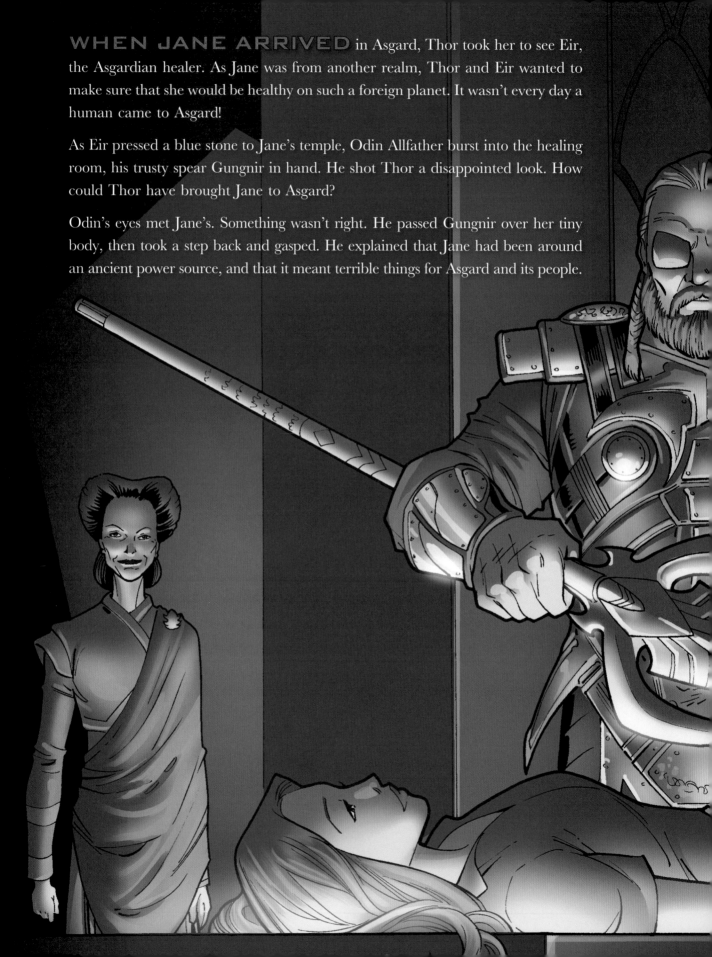

WHEN JANE ARRIVED in Asgard, Thor took her to see Eir, the Asgardian healer. As Jane was from another realm, Thor and Eir wanted to make sure that she would be healthy on such a foreign planet. It wasn't every day a human came to Asgard!

As Eir pressed a blue stone to Jane's temple, Odin Allfather burst into the healing room, his trusty spear Gungnir in hand. He shot Thor a disappointed look. How could Thor have brought Jane to Asgard?

Odin's eyes met Jane's. Something wasn't right. He passed Gungnir over her tiny body, then took a step back and gasped. He explained that Jane had been around an ancient power source, and that it meant terrible things for Asgard and its people.

ALTHOUGH THE NEWS WAS NOT GOOD, Jane still wanted to explore the Asgardian palace.

Thor took Jane to the palace's Hall of Science. Jane looked like a kid in a candy shop. Her eyes glistened as she drank in everything she saw. As they passed a large Asgardian tree, Jane was awestruck. She put her hands out to touch it and beams of light rolled off her fingers.

Suddenly, there was a loud *BONG!* It was a sound unlike anything Jane had ever heard before, and it rang throughout the Hall of Science. Everyone within the hall stopped and turned to stare at the Earthling. Lowering her head to hide her embarrassment, Jane quickly realized that the sound meant *Don't touch*. She quietly folded her hands behind her back and walked on with Thor.

Despite all this, Jane was having the time of her life. She was on Asgard and she was with Thor!

THOR AND JANE met with Odin. He explained the dark energy that Jane had contacted and how dangerous it was. Pointing to a picture of a Dark Elf leading an army, he told them of the birth of light.

"Some believe that before the universe there was nothing." He looked at Jane and Thor with a growing concern. "They are wrong. Before the universe there was darkness." Odin explained that Malekith built a weapon out of the darkness, and with it waged wars against the Nine Realms.

Eventually, the Asgardians prevailed and defeated Malekith, banishing him and his people from the universe. No one had seen or heard from them—until the dark energy showed up around Jane.

Jane and Thor walked around the royal palace. Jane reflected on her current situation. She was surrounded by a beautiful, strange world and was also learning about a dark force within the cosmos.

THEY MET FRIGGA, who grabbed Jane's hand and whisked her away. They had a lot to discuss, especially regarding Thor. Jane turned and smiled at the prince of Asgard. But what should have been a happy moment turned into a nightmare. A horn blew in the distance. It was the prisoners! They had broken out of their cells!

"Go," said Frigga to Thor. "I will look after her."

Thor nodded and blasted off into the sky toward the prison. Thor landed in front of the prison and raced down to the dungeon where he confronted the beasts. "Lay down your arms and return to your cells. You have my word; no harm will come to you."

A muscular Marauder stepped forward and landed a huge punch to Thor's chin. Thor grabbed his jaw. "Very well," he said. "You do not have my word."

CRACK! Thor slugged the Marauder with Mjolnir and sent him flying through a wall! The battle was on!

While the Asgardian warriors battled the prisoners, Heimdall heard the commotion from his post at the rainbow bridge and raced off toward the palace. But something wasn't right. He felt something behind him, up in the sky.

He tried to make out what was, and realized that whatever it was, it was invisible! But it soon started to part the clouds and take shape.

Heimdall leaped toward the invisible mass. With his swords out he plunged them deep into the side of the distortion. *BOOM!* There was a loud explosion.

It is a ship! Heimdall thought as it began to materialize before him. Heimdall attacked the vessel again with his swords, finally causing it to crash before him. But it wasn't the only craft. In fact, right behind it a massive mother ship appeared before his eyes. Suddenly, a door on the side of the ship opened and a smaller aircraft dropped out and raced toward the palace!

Heimdall watched, concern on his face.

ASGARD WAS UNDER ATTACK! Odin suited up to battle and protect his palace from the coming invasion. Odin ordered his warriors, "Send a squadron to the weapons vault. Defend it at all costs. Secure the dungeon."

When Frigga and Jane saw Odin heading off to battle, Frigga grew concerned, but Odin reassured his wife that it was just a small skirmish and it would all be fine.

Frigga wanted to believe Odin, but she wasn't a stranger to battles and she knew Odin wasn't being honest. As Odin left, Lady Sif and a squad of Einherjar trailed behind. Frigga and Jane watched them go off to battle, unsure of what was to come.

As dozens of evil Dark Elves tried to break into the palace, the Einherjar attempted to fight them off. The elves' lifeless eyes gave piercing looks to the Einherjar, but didn't intimidate them. They were armed and ready to defend Asgard.

But then their leader Malekith appeared. Walking through the middle of the battle, he remained calm. He looked at the throne of Asgard and fired his Dark Elf weapon at it, which instantly destroyed the once-magnificent seat of the king of Asgard. He let out a smile. Malekith was on the hunt to find and destroy anything that stood in his way.

While Malekith and his Dark Elves fought in the palace, the monster known as Kurse was decimating the Einherjar army.

MALEKITH burst into Frigga's chamber. Frigga immediately took out her sword, ready to defend her palace, as Jane hid behind her.

"Who are you?" she asked him.

"I am Malekith, and I will have what is mine!" he demanded. He took a step toward Jane, but Frigga swung her sword at him, slashing his cheek.

Frigga backed Malekith against the wall, and put her sword to his throat. Just when she thought she was in control, Frigga felt a dark and large presence behind her. Before Frigga could turn to see what it was, the enormous beast known as Kurse knocked her sword away and wrapped its gigantic arms around her throat.

Frigga gasped for air. She needed help. But Thor was too busy fighting Dark Elves throughout the palace. Things were looking grim for Frigga.

Just then, the King of Asgard burst through Frigga's chamber doors. His face was full of rage as he saw the beast holding his beloved wife.

"Frigga!" Odin called out, as Gungnir cracked with white energy.

As Malekith interrogated Frigga on the whereabouts of the dark energy, Odin screamed for him to release her.

But Malekith told Odin that he would only release Frigga if they gave him the dark energy, and Odin would have to choose between his world and his wife.

As Odin closed his eyes and faced his reality, the Mighty Thor burst into the chambers and hurled his mighty hammer at the Dark Elves!